War Dog Heroes

True Stories of Dog Courage in Wartime

by Jeannette Sanderson

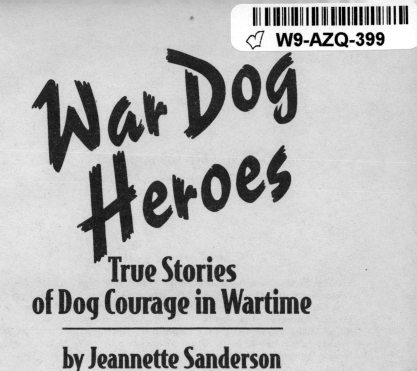

AN
APPLE
PAPERBACK

SCHOLASTIC INC.
New York Toronto London Auckland Sydney

Dedicated to the memory of
Marianne Oranczak Somers

Interior Photo Credits

Stubby: *Smithsonian Institution;* **WWI trench war dog:** *Archive Photos;* **"Dogs for Defense" poster:** *Hoover Institute Archives, Stanford University;* **Coastguardsman and guard dog, Caesar receives a message, Caesar wounded, War dog in training, Attack on command, Sentry duty, Chips meets General Eisenhower, Devildogs, Sled dogs in training;** *National Archives;* **Andy:** *National Archives/US Marine Corps;* **Nemo:** *Detroit Free Press.*

ISBN 0-590-50954-3

12 11 10 9 8 7 6 5 4   9/9 0 1 2/0

Printed in the U.S.A.   40

First Scholastic printing, April 1997

Acknowledgments

I would like to thank the many people who helped me write this book.

Lots of people helped me collect the resources I needed. The librarians at the Field Library in Peekskill, New York, were especially helpful. They got me books I needed from around the country. Peggy Whitlow of the U.S. Military Working Dog Institute at Lackland Air Force Base provided me with a great deal of information and cheerfully answered countless inquiries. Louise Arnold-Friend of the U.S. Military History Institute provided me with valuable historical information. Others whom I would like to thank for their help include R. M. Browning, Jr., a historian with the U.S. Coast Guard; Alan C. Aimone, Assistant Librarian for the Special Collections Division at the U.S. Military Academy Library at West Point; the people at the Pentagon Library; the National Archives; and the Smithsonian Institution.

I would also like to thank the people who helped me in ways that go beyond writing — Helen O'Reilly, Maria Johnson, and Kimberly Ferris.

I would like to thank Alice Sherman-Quine for her invaluable advice and encouragement.

And, finally, I would like to thank my family for their constant support.

Contents

War Dog Heroes

"Cry havoc and let slip the dogs of war." (William Shakespeare, English writer, 1564–1616)

The soldier took off to deliver an urgent message. He tore through tall, thick, sharp-edged grass. He ducked the rain of enemy fire. He plunged into and swam across a river. He leapt over a barbed-wire fence. He landed in a foxhole and delivered the message. During his dangerous mission, this soldier showed intelligence, bravery, strength, and loyalty. Who was he? He was Sandy, a dog who served with the United States Marines in World War II.

Sandy is but one in a long line of four-footed soldiers. The traits of most dogs — extraordinary senses of hearing and smell, loyalty, intelligence, speed, and coordination — have made them of great value to men at war for thousands of years.

War dogs are pictured in ancient Egyptian wall writing, thought by some to date back to 4000 B.C.

Cambyses, King of Persia, unleashed large packs of ferocious dogs on the Egyptians in 526 B.C. Less than five hundred years later, ancient Britain used mastiffs — large, barrel-chested dogs — in its fight against Caesar's invading army. Famous warriors Attila the Hun (A.D. 406–453) and Genghis Khan (A.D. 1162–1227) also used dogs in their conquests.

Some dogs were even outfitted for their battles. During the Middle Ages, war dogs were dressed in coats of mail, or armor, like the knights beside them. They wore spiked iron collars. This armor helped protect the dogs against the enemy's shower of spears and arrows.

Other dogs wore collars with long, curving steel blades. These tore into enemy soldiers and their horses. Some war dogs had vases strapped to their backs. The vases were filled with a flammable substance and set ablaze during battle. This sent the enemy's horses into a panic.

Not all early war dogs were fighting dogs. Some served in the equally important post of sentry, or guard dog.

Moustache

One of the most famous war dogs in history served as a sentry with the French in the Napoleonic Wars (1800–1815). His name was Moustache, and he was a three-time hero for his country.

Moustache first earned his stripes in 1800, when Napoleon's troops were camped near the Valley of Babo, Italy. It was night, and Moustache was standing guard as his masters slept. Suddenly he started barking wildly, rousing the French soldiers. They woke just in time to fight off a surprise attack by an Austrian regiment.

On another occasion, Moustache went into a frenzy when a messenger visited the camp. The dog growled at him, bared his fangs, and had to be restrained by guards to keep from attacking. Why was Moustache so upset by an innocent messenger? Because the man was not as innocent as he looked. In fact, he was a spy disguised as a messenger. The French troops realized this shortly after the man had left the camp. They immediately sent Moustache after him. The dog quickly tracked down the turncoat and helped bring him back to camp.

Moustache secured his reputation as a hero during an especially difficult battle for the French — the Battle of Austerlitz. There were a lot of casualties, but, thanks to Moustache, the French flag wasn't one of them.

An Austrian soldier had just killed the French flag-bearer. He was taking the muddy, torn flag from the dead man's hands when Moustache came to its defense. Moustache leapt straight for the enemy's throat. The Austrian dropped the flag and Moustache quickly picked it up. Then, with the pole in his mouth and the flag streaming in the air, the dog tore across the battlefield to return the cherished symbol to his company. This last act of bravery earned Moustache a special commendation from Napoleon's field marshal, Lannes.

Only death ended the patriotic dog's service to his country. Moustache was later killed on the battlefield.

World War I

"This is no dog. This is a war hero." (World War I veteran Corporal J. Robert Conroy, describing his dog, Stubby)

Machine guns. Tanks. Powerful shells. Poison gas. These were the weapons of World War I. What place did dogs have in twentieth century warfare? None, answered some military men at the start of the 1914–1918 conflict. These men couldn't see how dogs could survive, let alone serve, in the midst of these modern weapons. Did modern warfare make the war dog useless?

It soon became clear that the answer to that question was a booming no. In fact, World War I saw the first large-scale use of military dogs in history. But most of the seventy-five thousand or so dogs that served during this conflict were different from Moustache and war dogs of earlier days. Modern war created the need for modern war dogs.

Germany was the first country to fully appreciate the value of dogs in modern warfare. As early as 1885, the Germans began to train dogs in skills besides attack and defense. They trained thousands of dogs for messenger and sentry work. By the outset of World War I, Germany had trained more war dogs than any other nation. As many as thirty thousand trained war dogs fought for the Germans in World War I.

The French employed another twenty thousand trained war dogs in this conflict. Belgium, Italy, and England combined used another twenty-five thousand trained war dogs on the battlefield.

Dogs served many functions during this war. They were used as scouts, leading patrols and warning of ambush. They were used as sentries, guarding camps and supplies. They were used as messengers, carrying important information from headquarters to the front lines and back again. They were used as casualty or ambulance dogs, locating the wounded after battle. And they were used as draft and sledge dogs, carrying ammunition and other supplies across dangerous battlefields and over ice- and snow-covered mountains. During this war, one kennel of 150 Alaskan sled dogs moved more than 50 tons of supplies from the valley to the front line at the top of the mountain in just four days.

About seven thousand war dogs are thought to have lost their lives during World War I. To their countrymen, however, nearly all of the seventy-five thousand who served were heroes. Two of those heroes were Satan and Stubby.

Satan

Satan was one of the first modern war dog heroes. This French messenger dog made history when he saved a town and its garrison during World War I.

The battle at Verdun in northeast France had been raging for months. The French had taken, lost, and retaken the garrison at the small but important town of Thiaumont sixteen times. This last time several hundred French troops had dug in and were under orders to hold on until they were relieved.

It soon looked as if they were going to fight to their deaths. The French troops were running out of ammunition, but the enemy had no such problem. The Germans fired shell after shell into the falling fortress. Under steady attack and with little to defend themselves, many French soldiers were being killed or badly wounded.

Most of the enemy fire was coming from a German outfit off to the left. The beseiged soldiers knew that if they could make headquarters aware of the position of that battery, they might make it. But how could they send word? Telephone and telegraph lines had been cut. The last homing pigeon had been shot out of the air. Several soldiers had tried to make it through gunfire and enemy lines but had failed. It seemed there was no hope.

Except for Satan. The jet-black mongrel was fast. He had inherited speed from his father, a champion English greyhound. He was also intelligent — a trait he had inherited from his mother, a working Scotch collie. He was also fearless under fire, as he had shown during many earlier runs.

But there was one problem. Satan was at headquarters. His master, Duval, and the other men who needed him were at Thiaumont. If only headquarters would send them the dog!

The men at Verdun headquarters were preparing to do just that. It was clear to these men that their comrades at Thiaumont were in trouble. They had not heard from them for days. And the constant sound of gunfire in the distance was not reassuring. They knew the French troops' ammunition could not have lasted this long. The Germans could be the only source of all that gunfire. And their unarmed men had to be the target. Headquarters had to reestablish communications with Thiaumont before it was too late.

One of the officers ordered that Satan be given a chance to get through to the garrison. He was a good messenger, and he loved no one like his master. If anyone could make the trip, Satan could.

The men from headquarters put a message collar around Satan's neck. They wrote a note to their fellow soldiers and inserted it into the metal tube on the collar. Then they strapped baskets holding two carrier pigeons to the dog's back. Just then the gas alarm sounded. The men quickly fitted Satan with one of their own gas masks. Then they patted the dog on the back and sent him on his way.

Satan must have sensed that this trip was more dangerous than any he'd made before. He didn't dart off in his usual manner. Instead, he took slow, careful steps. He crouched close to the ground. He avoided enemy fire by hiding behind bushes and piles of dirt.

The brave dog moved in this careful fashion for the first mile and a half of his journey. Then he reached the final stretch. The garrison was in sight. Satan was just a half-mile away from his master.

At this point, Satan's mission became even more dangerous. There were no more bushes or piles of dirt for the dog to hide behind. The last half-mile he had to cover was all open land. Satan crouched and surveyed what lay ahead of him. Then he rose and started to run. A steady stream of gunfire poured at him from all directions.

At the garrison, Duval was scanning the smoke-filled barren stretch before him. Suddenly, he spotted something.

"*Voilà!* Satan! Satan!" he called, jumping up.

His fellow soldiers trained their eyes and hopes on the black speck in the distance. Was it really Satan? they wondered. His head looked so funny, and he appeared to have wings.

The dog continued racing toward his master. But as he leapt through the air a German bullet caught him in the leg. The men watching from the garrison gasped as they saw their hopes stumble and fall. The dog quickly dragged himself back to his feet. But he was disoriented, and seemed unsure about what to do next.

Duval knew his dog needed help. The man stood and, in full view of the enemy and the enemy's bullets, waved his arms and shouted.

"Satan! Satan! Come, *mon ami!* For France! For . . . !" A bullet silenced him.

But Satan had heard his master's call. He ran toward the fallen man on three legs, the fourth hanging loosely at the hip. In this way, he made it to the fort.

Once there, welcoming soldiers pulled the message from the tube on his collar.

"FOR GOD'S SAKE, HOLD ON. WILL SEND TROOPS TO RELIEVE YOU TOMORROW."

The men wondered how they would last until the next day. Then they noticed that what had appeared to be wings on Satan's shoulders were in fact baskets carrying homing pigeons.

An officer grabbed a piece of paper. He quickly wrote "Stop the German battery on our left." He added some figures showing the battery's exact location. He copied the message onto another piece of paper. Then he put the messages into the aluminum capsules on the legs of each of the homing pigeons.

The men then tossed both birds into the air. They watched them circle once before flying toward headquarters. The Germans shot and killed one bird before it flew out of sight. The French soldiers could only hope and pray that the other bird would not meet a similar end.

When they heard the burst of gunfire behind the German batallion twenty minutes later, they knew the second bird had made it home. Within an hour, the French had silenced the German battery and won Thiaumont. It was clear Satan had saved the day.

Satan's leg was repaired and he retired from the French Army a hero. The dog had lost his master, but he had saved an entire town.

Stubby

The United States had no official war dog program during World War I. But a number of American dogs still found their way to the front. Some simply kept the soldiers company. Some saved their fellow Americans' lives. Stubby did both.

The bull terrier with the stubby tail appeared out of nowhere in 1916 to join students doing military training at Yale Field. Day after day he trotted among the group as they performed their drills. His friendliness was contagious, and before long the boys adopted the chunky dog as their own.

When orders came to move on to Newport News for final training, the boys didn't know what to do. They couldn't leave Stubby behind. But they couldn't very well put him in uniform and bring him along either. Regulations clearly stated that dogs were not allowed in the military.

They decided to ask Corporal J. Robert Conroy, who was going down to Newport News in a supply car, to hide the dog in with the supplies. Conroy didn't like the idea of smuggling a dog. Then he met Stubby. The dog licked the corporal's face until the man forgot his resistance to the idea. Conroy hid the dog under the equipment and set out for Newport News.

The boys and their dog weren't there long before they got orders to sail for France. Now Conroy, too, worried about leaving Stubby behind.

The morning they were to set sail, Conroy and Stubby befriended the Military Police (MP) officer where their ship was docked. Conroy quickly secured the soldier's help in smuggling Stubby aboard ship.

Stubby spent the next year and a half on the front lines with Conroy. The friendly dog proved himself both fearless and loyal during at least nineteen battles. He saved countless lives.

Because of his extraordinary senses of hearing and smell, Stubby was able to give warning signals to his men. The dog heard the whine of shells long before his troops did. When he hurled himself to the ground and covered his head with his paws, the soldiers knew they should also take cover.

Stubby also smelled the enemy's poison gas before his fellow soldiers got a whiff of it. During the first such attack, Stubby tore through the trenches, barking wildly and waking everyone. The men figured out what was happening in time to put on their gas masks.

Stubby was so busy giving the warning, however, that he didn't get himself to safety in time. Conroy had to rush the poisoned dog to the base hospital. He quickly recovered and rejoined his troops. Conroy, meanwhile, tried to order or even make a gas mask for Stubby, to protect him against future attacks. He never had any luck, though. None of the masks could be made to fit the dog's blunt muzzle.

The dog was fearless under fire and would work the battlefield to try to comfort fallen soldiers. He would lick their mud-stained faces to try to wash away the pain. Then he would go find more professional help. Stubby's efforts brought help to seriously wounded men who might otherwise have been left for dead.

Stubby performed many other brave deeds. One of the most dramatic occurred during a seemingly peaceful night as Stubby slept at his master's side.

Stubby must have heard something because his head jerked up, waking his master. Conroy opened his eyes to see Stubby sniffing the air. He must not have liked what he smelled, because he let out a low growl. Then he leapt out of the dugout and disappeared around a corner.

Conroy grabbed his rifle and quickly followed. He could hear the sounds of a struggle and then a loud, piercing cry. The lieutenant turned the corner and stopped short when he saw the source of all the commotion. Stubby had captured a German spy — by the seat of his pants. The German was struggling to shake off his sharp-fanged foe. Conroy easily disarmed the distraught enemy. He had a tougher time convincing Stubby to release his great catch.

Stubby suffered several injuries during battle. His closest call came when a hand grenade landed just a few feet away from the dog and nearly killed him. The dog spent several weeks in the hospital where he hovered near death. But the boys hadn't seen the last of this brave soldier. His spirit wouldn't die. Stubby recovered and rejoined his troops six weeks later, in time for the next offensive.

Stubby's bravery did not go unnoticed. A group of Frenchwomen made him a hand-sewn coat decorated with Allied flags and a hero's medal. He was introduced to and "shook hands" with President Woodrow Wilson. General John J. Pershing awarded him a gold medal. The marines made him an honorary sergeant.

The dog was even decorated for a "civilian" act of bravery. It happened when he was with Conroy in Paris, France. The two were crossing the street one day when suddenly Stubby bolted, yanking the leash from Conroy's hand. The dog tore toward a girl who was standing on the corner. As he neared her he leapt up and knocked her out of the path of a careening taxi. The car just grazed both of them as it whizzed by.

Conroy and Stubby returned to the United States in 1919. Stubby lived the last seven years of his life as a retired hero. He attended American Legion conventions. He led parades. He even visited the White House — twice! In 1921 he was officially received by President Warren Harding, and in 1924 he was received by President Calvin Coolidge.

A clerk at a famous New York City hotel once told Conroy that he would have to find a kennel for Stubby because dogs were not allowed at the hotel. The angered, retired corporal told the man, "This is no dog. This is a war hero." Stubby was invited to stay. He "signed" the guest book with his paw print.

When Stubby died in 1926 his body was stuffed and, along with his decorated coat, put on display at the Smithsonian Institution in Washington, D.C.

Dogs for Defense

"The value of dogs has been recognized and put to use by practically every nation except our own." (from an appeal for dogs by the U.S. Army to Hawaiian residents, 1942)

The United States was among the last of the world powers to accept the value of war dogs, despite the fact that the animals had been used during times of war throughout the nation's history.

Native Americans were the first Americans to use war dogs. They posted dogs outside sleeping camps to warn against enemies. They also used dogs for transportation. The animals carried packs on their backs or were harnessed to and pulled travois, a carrying device on two poles.

These native people's need for sentry dogs increased after the arrival of Christopher Columbus and other explorers. These foreigners brought war dogs of their own, usually bloodhounds, and used them to hunt down Native Americans.

Nearly three hundred years later, Ben Franklin wanted to make dogs part of the militia during the American Revolution. He argued that the dogs' sharp hearing and sense of smell would help protect against British ambush. Although dogs never officially became part of the militia, the troops had a number of four-footed soldiers among them. Many of these had followed their masters to war. Others were strays adopted by the troops. These dogs often acted as sentries for their camps. Nearly one hundred years later, dogs played the same unofficial role during the Civil War.

One of the first official records of an American dog being used as a scout during war occurred during the Spanish American War (1898). Captain Steel of the American Cavalry used a dog named Don to lead his troops through the jungle in Cuba. The Captain had nothing but praise for Don, claiming that the dog's presence prevented his troops from being ambushed. Steel later said:

> "Dogs are the only scouts that can secure a small detachment against ambuscade in these tropical jungles. The bush is so dense and the trails are so crooked and over such rough territory that the leading man at one or two hundred yards is out of sight of the main party. The insurgents lying in ambush often let the leading man pass by and open with a vol-

ley upon the wagons and the main party of the escort."

Captain Steel's words were echoed in later wars. But at the time they weren't enough to convince the United States government to begin a war dog program. A bill to create a contingent of war dogs was introduced to Congress during World War I, but failed to pass.

At the outset of World War II (1939–1945), the only dogs employed by the United States Army were the sled dogs used by the infantry in Alaska. Then the Japanese attacked Pearl Harbor on December 7, 1941. This event led to the formation of the first official war dog program in the United States.

Roland Kilbon, who wrote about dogs, was sitting at his desk not long after this deadly surprise attack when the telephone rang.

"The dog game must play its part in this thing," said the voice on the other end of the line. It was Mrs. Milton S. Erlanger, a noted breeder of poodles, who was very active in the dog world. "Other countries have used dogs in their armies for years and ours has not. We've got to do it. Just think what dogs can do guarding forts, munition plants, and other such places."

Kilbon agreed. He and Mrs. Erlanger met to discuss establishing an organization that would promote war dogs. They invited other prominent dog people to their meetings. By early 1942, Dogs for Defense, Inc., an organization that would unite dog people, clubs, breeders, and pet owners in finding and financing dogs for the Army, was born.

"We all were certain that it was a great cause," Kilbon says of Dogs for Defense. But the dog fanciers had their work cut out for them. Before they could begin fundraising, recruiting, and training, they had to convince a still-skeptical Army of the value of war dogs.

One officer who didn't need much convincing was Lieutenant Colonel Clifford C. Smith, chief of the plant protection branch of the Quartermaster Corps. He had been impressed by the work of several sentry dogs being used at supply depots on the West Coast. He went to talk to his chief, Major General Edmund B. Gregory, Quartermaster General, about his needs and how they might be met by dogs.

"General Gregory, sir," Colonel Smith said. "Now that our country is at war there is more danger than ever of sabotage at our Quartermaster supply depots. We need more protection, but there will be a problem getting additional guards.

"I've been looking into the possibility of using dogs as guards. I understand that a trained dog is better than three or even more men. I'd like your permission, sir, to try two hundred dogs as an experiment."

General Gregory agreed to Colonel Smith's request. On March 13, 1942, Dogs for Defense received the order for two hundred trained sentry dogs from the Army. It was the first time in the history of the United States that war dogs were officially recognized. Dogs for Defense readily accepted the assignment.

Under the leadership of Harry Caesar, a director of the American Kennel Club, Dogs for Defense had already set up specifications for training sentry dogs. They had lined up 402 dog clubs that were willing to provide dogs. And they had offers of service from a number of obedience trainers.

The first nine dogs recruited and trained by Dogs for Defense were sent to Brigadier General Philip S. Gage at Fort Hancock, New Jersey, in May 1942. The general was pleased with his new recruits. He reported that the dogs proved especially valuable during the night blackout, when their superior hearing more than compensated for the limited range of the human sentries' vision. The dogs also boosted the human soldiers' morale. They were good company for the men on what had been a solitary post.

Despite the growing number of people who believed that dogs had a place in the United States Army, there were still many who had to be convinced. A frightening event that took place in June 1942 helped persuade them.

Operation Pastorious

It happened around midnight. Twenty-one-year-old coast guardsman John C. Cullen was making his six-mile patrol from Amagansett Station on Long Island, New York, when someone approached him.

"Identify yourself," Cullen said to the figure cloaked in fog and darkness.

The man said his name was George Davis. "We're fishermen from Southampton and we ran aground here," he added.

Cullen tried to see through the fog. He could just make out that the man had three companions. One of them approached Davis and shouted something in a foreign language. Cullen thought it sounded like German.

"Shut up you damn fool!" the man who called himself Davis snapped at his companion.

This exchange made Cullen suspicious. The coast guardsman suggested that the group return with him to the Coast Guard station. "Davis" refused and began to threaten Cullen.

"I don't want to kill you," he said.

Then, for some unknown reason, Davis changed his approach. He took out a wad of bills and offered Cullen three hundred dollars to forget he had seen anything.

Cullen was armed only with a flashlight and a flare gun. He was outnumbered and didn't know if

21

these men carried weapons. He decided that the only way to escape unharmed was to pretend to accept the bribe. So he took the money and walked away. As soon as he was out of sight, he ran as fast as he could back to the Coast Guard station.

After hearing his story and seeing the money, the commanding officer of the Amagansett station armed Cullen and three other coast guardsmen. Then the group returned to the spot where Cullen had met Davis.

The four men were gone. But through the fog the coast guardsmen saw the dark hulking outline of a German submarine that had run aground. The coast guardsmen hid behind a dune and watched the U202 free itself and slip away.

The next morning the Coast Guard searched the beach and found explosives and incendiary devices. They notified the United States Federal Bureau of Investigation (FBI) at once.

Within two weeks "George Davis," a German spy, and his three accomplices were in custody. These arrests led to the capture of four other German agents who had landed undetected on the Florida coast a few days after their compatriots had run aground in New York.

It turned out that the eight agents were on a special mission called Operation Pastorious (named after the first German immigrant to America). The men had been given a crash course in sabotage and divided into two teams. Each team had been given explosives and ninety thousand dollars in United States currency for bribes and other expenses. Then each had shipped out on their respective U-boats for the United States. Once there, their instructions were to bomb factories and railroads. Their primary goal was to create panic and disrupt transportation.

These were dangerous enemy agents. What would have happened if Cullen had not been at the exact spot where the U-boat landed that night? What would have happened if the German spy had decided to shoot the unarmed coast guardsman? The frightening answers inspired by these questions underscored the need for better security not only along the coasts but also at industrial plants and army installations throughout the country. They also added to the growing interest in the use of war dogs, especially for sentry duty.

Lieutenant Commander McClelland Barclay of the U.S. Naval Reserve was a strong proponent of using dogs to help patrol U.S. coasts. He argued, "Unless we adopt something of this sort for our defense, it will be very difficult to prevent the landings of enemy agents at all points of our coastline."

The Coast Guard heeded Barclay's advice. By the end of 1942, it made the following announcement: "The latest allies employed by coast guardsmen in their constant watch along American shores are trained dogs."

By the end of World War II, more than nine thousand trained sentry dogs had stood post along the U.S. coastline and at factories, military bases, and supply depots around the country.

Sacrifices
and Rewards

"Please accept my thanks for your unselfish con-tribution to our war effort." (Brigadier General Phillip S. Gage in a letter to ten-year-old Walter Laffer of Cleveland, Ohio, who had donated his dog, King, to Dogs for Defense)

Requests for dogs were pouring into Dogs for Defense headquarters. It became clear that this operation was going to be bigger than anyone expected. The Army's interest was expanding beyond sentry dogs. In July 1942, the Secretary of War directed General Gregory, the Quartermaster General, to broaden the scope of the war dog program. He wanted dogs trained for scout, messenger, and sled work, in addition to sentry duty. General Gregory decided that the Army should take over the training of these dogs while leaving the recruiting to Dogs for Defense.

This was no minor task. Mrs. Milton Erlanger and William E. Buckley, legal counselor for Dogs for Defense, went to Washington to discuss the changes in the war dog program with General Gregory. When they returned to New York, they reported the results of this meeting to Harry Caesar, the organization's president.

"Well, Harry," Mr. Buckley said. "The Army wants lots of dogs."

"Good. Do you think as many as five hundred?"

Mr. Buckley laughed. "They want a great many more than that. They want thousands!"

Mr. Buckley wasn't exaggerating. On December 30, 1942, the Quartermaster General told Dogs for Defense that the United States Armed Forces would eventually need 125,000 dogs. That estimate would later be revised downward, but it was clear that Dogs for Defense had a big job to do.

The Army, Coast Guard, and Marines called their orders in to Dogs for Defense headquarters in New York City. This clearinghouse was busy. In mid-August 1943, for example, personnel from the Army's training center at Fort Robinson, Nebraska, called in an order. They wanted four hundred dogs every two weeks for the next two-and-a-half months. Another training center wanted one-hundred-fifty dogs every two weeks. At its peak, Dogs for Defense was shipping fifteen hundred dogs a month.

Dogs for Defense handled these orders by dividing them among its more than thirty regional offices throughout the United States. The directors of these offices were responsible for recruiting dogs from their areas. They did this by making speeches and placing newspaper and radio advertisements to try to convince dog owners that their dogs were badly needed for the war effort. They enlisted and inspected their new recruits. Then they shipped the dogs to training centers or returned them to their owners.

During its three years of operation, Dogs for Defense recruited nearly twenty thousand dogs. Many of them were purebred and worth a lot of money. It was estimated that the organization's efforts saved the government more than two million dollars — a conservative estimate of the dogs' total value.

But Dogs for Defense didn't do it all alone. They had a lot of help from a patriotic American public.

Like the directors, there were many people willing to volunteer their services. Drivers from the Red Cross and the American Women's Voluntary Service transported dogs; veterinarians examined the dogs free of charge; kennel clubs gave shows to raise money; show owners donated crates and dog food; and ordinary citizens made speeches, performed clerical work, and ran errands, all to help supply war dogs to America's armed forces.

Then, of course, there were those men, women, and children who made the greatest sacrifices of all — their beloved dogs.

Nine-year-old Ralph H. Hallenbeck, Jr., of Baldwin, Long Island (New York), went to his father one day and told him he was going to enlist in the marines. The boy wanted to serve his country just as his father had as a Marine Corps officer during World War I.

Mr. Hallenbeck told Ralph he was too young to join the marines. "Perhaps you can do something else that will help," he suggested.

Ralph thought about his. He had been reading about dogs being used in the war effort. Topper, his three-year-old Doberman pinscher, had been with them since he was two months old. Ralph hated to think about parting with him. He was a member of the family. But he also was sure that Topper was just what the marines were looking for.

The young boy went to his father a few days later and suggested that Topper represent the Hallenbecks in this war. The father agreed and Topper became a marine. (Topper's record shows he represented the Hallenbecks well: He won a commendation for alerting his troops to enemy patrols and ambushes.)

The Hawthorn Barracks of Troop K, New York State Police, sent four of their rare and famed bloodhounds to war through Dogs for Defense.

An ex-governor and chief justice of the Supreme Court sent his only pet to serve in the Armed Forces.

Metropolitan Opera star Ezio Pinza sent his two Dalmatians, Boris and Figaro, to the army. Along with them he sent an album of his operatic recordings. "If they get lonesome, play one of these records for them," he asked.

These recruits, among thousands sent to Dogs for Defense from all over the country, were their owners' free and unconditional gifts. All owners made the sacrifice knowing that they might never see their beloved pets again. And, even if their dogs did survive the war, Dogs for Defense made no promise to return them to their owners after the war was over.

In recognition of their sacrifices, dog donors received certificates expressing the gratitude of the United States government. But their real reward was the knowledge that they had done their best to help the war effort. The dogs they sent to war might save soldiers' lives.

Caesar

Such thoughts helped the Glazers say goodbye to their three-year-old German shepherd, Caesar.

"We all had tears in our eyes," said Irving, the youngest of the three Glazer brothers.

With the two oldest Glazer boys in the army and Irving headed for the Merchant Marine, Mr. and

Mrs. Glazer were already giving a lot to their country. But when they read an appeal from Dogs for Defense, they knew that the big, intelligent, black-and-grey dog could save the life of someone's son, someone's brother, so they had to let him go.

The family of Private Rufus Mayo would be forever grateful. Mayo of Montgomery, Alabama, and Private John Kleeman of Philadelphia, Pennsylvania, were the two young marines assigned to Caesar at Camp Lejeune in North Carolina. Caesar had been trained as a messenger dog. In battle, his job would be to deliver messages between his two handlers when there were no other means of communication between headquarters and the front lines.

Both young men were crazy about Caesar. They wrote to their families about the champion they had been assigned. Mayo wrote that he thought Caesar had more sense than the average man and that he would "not give Caesar up for a general's commission." He thought of Caesar as a member of the family and had the dog send his love by putting his paw mark on the lower right-hand corner of every letter he sent home.

Kleeman wrote to his family that he wanted to bring Caesar home during furlough to show him off. But he never got a chance to do that. He and the rest of the First Marine Dog Platoon were shipped to Camp Pendleton, California, and then to the South Pacific.

The platoon was under heavy shellfire from the moment it arrived at Bougainville in the Solomon Islands on D day, November 1, 1943. Mayo and Caesar were assigned to Company M, which soon advanced further than any other company in the enemy-infested jungle.

Once there, however, the company had trouble sending word back to the battalion command post. The soldiers' walkie-talkies failed in the dense jungle. Phone lines hadn't yet been laid. Caesar quickly became the only link between those on the front line and the command group in the rear.

On day one, Caesar made several trips between Company M and the battalion command post. He made these trips in bad light and under enemy fire.

By day two, the marines had managed to stretch a telephone line between the front position and headquarters. When the Japanese cut this line, Caesar again became the only means of communication between the two posts. Once more he braved sniper fire to carry messages that could mean life or death.

Caesar's courage over these two days proved he was an exceptional messenger. But it wasn't as a messenger that Caesar earned his fame and the gratitude of the Rufus family. It was as a watchdog that Caesar really saved the day.

It was the second night of the invasion. Lieutenant Clyde Henderson, commander of the First Marine Dog Platoon, asked Mayo to sleep with Caesar in a foxhole several hundred yards forward of the rest of the company.

Henderson later explained that it was harrowing to try to sleep in a foxhole when you were wondering if the enemy might creep in and knife you while you slept. The enemy "had been devils at infiltrating outposts at night," Henderson said, "so we placed dogs to supplement the human sentries."

This tactic paid off at dawn the next day. A sharp movement woke Mayo in time to see Caesar leaping out of the foxhole. Mayo quickly called him back. Just as the obedient dog turned around, a Japanese soldier pumped two bullets into him.

Henderson describes what followed:

"During the confusion of battle Caesar disappeared. Mayo was frantic. He called me to learn whether I had seen him. He was half shouting and half crying. I hadn't seen Caesar. Soon we found a trail of blood through the jungle . . ."

The trail led back to the command post. It ended in some bushes near Private Kleeman. That's where the barely conscious dog had collapsed when he tried to drag himself back to his other handler, and safety.

When Mayo saw his dog, he "ran and lay down beside him and hugged him gently," Henderson says.

Three marines quickly made a special stretcher for their fallen hero. They chopped down two long poles and two short poles and fastened them together. Then they fitted this frame with a blanket and placed the wounded dog upon it.

One dozen marines volunteered to carry Caesar's stretcher to the first-aid station. Other marines saluted as the wounded hero was carried by.

Mayo and Kleeman waited anxiously outside the hospital tent. After twenty minutes the surgeon came out. He told them that he had removed one bullet but could not remove the other. It was too close to Caesar's heart. Still, the surgeon thought the strong dog would pull through.

He was right. Caesar was back on active duty after just three weeks.

In a personal letter to the Glazers, General Thomas Holcomb, commandant of the Marine Corps, thanked the family for volunteering Caesar and praised the dog for "saving the lives of many marines."

Dogs and Dollars

"Give Dogs and Dollars." (Dogs for Defense slogan)

Dogs for Defense was committed to providing the best available dogs to the Army, Coast Guard, and Marines without cost to the government. Although the dogs were gifts from the American public, Dogs for Defense still had to pay to enlist, inspect, and ship the dogs to induction centers. The organization kept its expenses down to about seven dollars a dog by using as many volunteers as possible. But even this small amount added up, especially when Dogs for Defense was shipping as many as fifteen hundred dogs a month. It was clear that Dogs for Defense needed dogs *and* dollars.

The organization raised money in much the same way that it recruited dogs — with posters, speeches, radio appeals, and newspaper and magazine articles. But its most successful fund-raising idea came from James M. Austin, owner of Saddler, one of the most outstanding show dogs of all time. The idea was known as the War Dog Fund.

This fund raised money by selling honorary ranks in all branches of the services to stay-at-home dogs. These dogs might be too small, too large, too old, too young, or too needed at home to be able to join the K-9 Corps. But now their owners could have the satisfaction of helping in this war effort.

The cost would range from one dollar for a private or seaman to $100 for a general or admiral. With Dog for Defense's approval, Austin sent letters to 125 of his dog-fancying friends urging them to enlist their pets. He received 112 applications, 54 of which were for admirals or generals.

Following this success, Austin launched a nationwide campaign to recruit stay-at-home dogs. It was an instant success. Applications, letters, and money poured into the War Dog Fund's offices.

One farm boy wrote: "I am a boy nine years old. My dad fought in World War I. He is too old to go to this war and I am too young. We are helping at home in every way we can ... We have a very good helper, Top, my dog. He helps us get the cows to their place. Daddy says we could not do without him. Enclosed please find $1.00, one dollar, for which I wish to register my dog as a Soldier War Dog. Thank you."

One woman from Nebraska wrote: "I have two sons in the Army and we have a wire-haired terrier and he belongs to the boys. He was twelve years old last Friday, March 12. He is getting old and crabby and my sons say he would make a good tough crabby sergeant. So that is what they want him to be in the civilian army. His name is Rags."

One G.I. wrote from Africa: "If you will take the enclosed dollar and enroll a certain little dog named Ginger on your War Dog Roster and mail his membership tag to my wife you will contribute much to a soldier in Africa, who wants to please his home folks and let them know he is with them in all they do."

A marine captain wrote from somewhere in the Pacific: "Just read about your War Dog Fund. I think it is an excellent idea. In this lonesome outpost the numerous dogs are wonderful companions. My dog at home has helped make up my absence to my wife. Please enlist Toby as a private."

Some dogs even "wrote" to enlist themselves. This letter was from a dog named Sal who lived in Hawaii: "I am an English bulldog who is too old to get into this fight, but who still has the pep to take care of the house while the mistress works in a war plant and the old man builds factories. . . . I want to be a seaman because somewhere in the seven seas a couple of kids from my house are in the submarines that are knocking the spots off the Japanese and the Germans. . . . "

There was even an application from the White House. President Franklin D. Roosevelt sent one dollar and asked that Fala, his Scottie, be made a private in the Army.

Dogs were enlisted from every state in the union. Within fourteen months, the War Dog Fund had enlisted twenty-five thousand dogs and raised seventy-five thousand dollars for Dogs for Defense.

Pet to Private

"Concrete punishment and reward ... may be necessary on occasion, but ... it is more pleasant and more convenient to rely, so far as possible, upon the dog's eagerness to serve." (War Department Technical Manual 10-396: *War Dogs*, July 1, 1943)

Suppose you had wanted to donate *your* dog to Dogs for Defense. Before you started imagining it performing all sorts of brave deeds, you had to make sure it met certain standards. It had to be the right age — between fourteen months and three-and-a-half years; the right height — between twenty-three and twenty-eight inches at the shoulder; and the right weight — between fifty-five and eighty-five pounds. It didn't have to be purebred, though that helped. Males were favored over females. Your dog also had to be alert, muscular, and healthy.

If you had a dog that fit this bill, and thousands did, your next step would be to fill out a questionnaire giving breed, shoulder height, age, call name, sex, and American Kennel Club name and number (if applicable). You would also be asked about your dog's overall health, temperament, and whether it was gun- or storm-shy.

Dogs for Defense would then review this questionnaire. If your dog looked good on paper, Dogs for Defense would have a veterinarian examine it to make sure it looked as good in the flesh. Your dog would be tested to see if it could stand loud noises. More than half of the dogs brought into Dogs for Defense were disqualified for service when they failed the physical exam and/or the noise test.

If your dog managed to pass, congratulations! It would be inducted into the armed forces. As a new canine recruit, it would be sent to one of several dog-training centers around the country. Once there, a vet would examine it for illness and injury. It would be given a painless serial tattoo either inside its left flank or inside its left ear. Then it would be placed in an isolation cage and observed for two weeks. If it still appeared healthy at the end of that period, your dog would be assigned to a student handler.

Most handlers were dog owners and had a fair amount of experience with dogs. They were generally intelligent and patient, two traits needed to train dogs.

While your dog was in isolation, its handler would be learning the basics of dog care. He would learn proper grooming: massage and brush fur, don't bathe too often, clip nails, bathe eyes daily, clean teeth and ears, look out for fleas and ticks. He would learn proper feeding: a well-balanced diet of meat, grains, and vegetables, but no bones, to be fed once a day, and only by the handler. He would learn the importance of keeping a dog's kennel clean. And he would learn first aid.

Before beginning basic training, the handler would give your dog a chain-choke collar. Whenever your dog wore this, it would be on duty. When it wore its leather kennel collar, it would be off duty. Your dog would soon know what was expected of it based on what collar it was wearing.

Then your dog and its handler would begin training together. From the outset, the trainer would make it clear that he was the master. He would groom, feed, exercise, pet, and praise the animal. No one else would be allowed to befriend your dog.

An event at a Boston, Massachusetts, exhibit of war dog training showed how well the dogs learned to obey a single master. A woman visiting the show recognized her dog, the dog she had given to Dogs for Defense, as one of the dogs in the training exhibit. She proudly pointed out her dog to the officer in charge. The officer invited her into the ring.

When the woman entered the ring, her dog saw her right away. He pricked his ears and started wagging his tail.

The officer asked the woman to call her dog. She did. But at the same time, the dog's handler told him to stay. The dog shook with self-restraint. But he didn't budge from the spot where he stood. When his proud handler softly told him, "Okay," the dog leapt across the ring and into his mistress's arms. After a short visit, the dog's handler called him back. The dog instantly obeyed. He clearly knew who was giving the orders now.

Your dog's first weeks would be spent in basic training. During this time, your dog would learn to obey both voice and arm signals. The latter were very important because there were instances where making a sound could cost a soldier his life. Your dog would learn the commands taught in civilian dog-obedience classes as well as those considered necessary in military situations.

Your dog would learn to "heel," or to walk on the left side of its trainer with its right ear and shoulder at the trainer's left knee. This would leave the soldier's shooting arm free.

Your dog would learn the commands "Sit" and "Down." Your dog would also learn the commands "Stay," "Come," and "Crawl." If your dog was like most, it would have a tough time learning to crawl. But it had to master this exercise in order to survive under fire. Your dog would also be taught to "jump" and by the end of training would probably be able to scale an eight-and-a-half-foot wall.

Your dog and its handler would regularly run an

obstacle course. Your dog would crawl under wire, walk along shaky boards, creep through tunnels, swim across wide streams, and leap over barricades, among other things. This would strengthen it and develop confidence in its abilities.

During this period of basic training your dog would practice wearing a muzzle and a gas mask. It would ride in trucks with other dogs and learn to do so without fighting or getting carsick, both causes for rejection from the armed services.

Your dog would be tested under fire. At the marine's Camp Lejeune War Dog Training Company, dogs and their handlers were required to crawl through smoke screens while officers hurled explosives in their direction. Many dogs would try to bolt during the first of these half-hour exercises. But their handlers would hold them down with a protective arm and talk softly to them. By the third or fourth such exercise, most dogs and handlers became accustomed to the simulated battlefront conditions.

Many dogs were weeded out during this period of basic training. Dogs that were gun-shy, oversensitive, playful, forgetful, or that didn't get along with other dogs were rejected. Some dogs were even rejected because they were too friendly.

Fritz, a five-year-old German shepherd that belonged to Clifford H. Lee of Atlantic City, New Jersey, was one such dog. The army flunked Fritz from its K-9 Corps training course at Gulfport,

Mississippi, because he was too good-natured to be a canine soldier. Most dogs, when provoked during training, bared their teeth and tried to attack. Not Fritz. The dog just wagged his tail, "from the nose back." Fritz didn't have an ounce of the aggression needed to be a good soldier.

If your dog wasn't a major tail-wagger and successfully completed basic training, he was considered ready for specialized training. Only the most intelligent, willing, sensitive, and energetic dogs would be trained as scouts, messengers, and casualty dogs (twelve weeks). The rest would be trained as sentries (eight weeks).

Sentry Dogs

A sentry was basically a guard dog. It was trained to bark, growl, or silently indicate the approach or presence of strangers. It was taught to attack on command. A trainer in padded clothing would shout at the dog, wave a stick at its nose, or make other threatening gestures. The dog's handler would encourage the dog to attack.

The dog would be taught to bite and release on command. It would be taught to go for the enemy's right arm. This was usually the "weapon arm," since the majority of people are right-handed. The dog would practice lunging, biting, and releasing on a soldier whose arm was well wrapped in bandage, inner-tubing, and leather strips.

The dog was subjected to repeated mock attacks by different "enemies." Soon the dog grew to trust no one but its master. The dog would learn to be on the lookout for strangers whenever its master said, "Watch him."

Scout Dogs

A scout dog was trained to work with combat units and to give silent warning as to the presence of strangers. Much of its initial training was the same as that used for sentry dogs. An important exception was the stress on silence for scout dogs. In the field, any sound could draw the attention of the enemy. So a scout dog was trained to alert, or give warning, silently, and was scolded if he barked or growled.

Each dog had its own way of alerting. Some dogs raised the hair on their backs. Some perked up their ears or curled their tails. Some dogs moved faster or slower. Some dogs stood still, others lay down. Each handler had to learn how his dog alerted.

"In general, it may be said that through all his training, the man gives orders to his dog," said Captain Jackson Boyd, commander of the Marine's war dog training camp. But, he added, "once trained, the dog gives orders to the man."

Scout dog training took battlefront conditions into account another way. The dogs were subjected to a good deal of training under gunfire. This was done to sharpen their senses of hearing and smell in spite of the loud and smoky distractions of battle.

Messenger Dogs

A messenger dog helped troops in the vital area of communication. It carried messages — requests for back-up or first aid, or amended maps — in a pouch on his neck. It strung telephone wire from a coil attached to its collar. It transported carrier pigeons in wicker cages on its back. And, when necessary, it served as a pack dog and carried as much as twenty-five pounds of emergency supplies.

Messengers were two-man dogs. One master would put a collar with a leather pouch or a metal tube around the dog's neck, then tell it to "report." The other master would call it. When the dog came to him he would praise it. Then he would tell the animal to "sit," while he removed the collar. The dog quickly learned that the collar meant it had to go from one handler to the other.

This dog's training would start with the dog reporting to a handler who was in plain sight about twenty feet away. Then it would report to a handler who had hidden. As training progressed, the dog would have to search as much as a mile to find its hidden handler. During this search it may have had to scale walls, swim rivers, dodge traffic, and duck gunfire, all to prepare it for real battlefront conditions.

Casualty Dogs

The casualty dog assisted the Medical Corps in locating wounded men that might otherwise be overlooked. These were men who were unconscious, buried under the debris of battle, or hiding for safety.

A casualty dog began training with a man, known as the casualty, lying on the ground six feet in front of it. The man would wordlessly try to get the dog to come to him. When it did, both the "casualty" and the dog's handler would praise it. The "casualty" would then get up and walk about fifty yards before falling again.

"Search," the dog's handler would tell it. This exercise would be repeated over greater distances, first during the day then at night. Finally, the dog would be required to find hidden "casualties."

These men would be wearing blood-stained clothes. They would hide in trenches, foxholes, and behind trees. Gunfire would be added to the exercises to test the dogs under battlefront conditions.

Whatever their field, all military working dogs received continuous training throughout their careers. Dogs that stopped training for just thirty days had drastically reduced capabilities. Some even had to be retrained.

On Guard

"I don't think there is a group of men anywhere in the world who are as attached to their dogs as the men of the dog patrol. You see, our very life might depend on our dogs. . . ." (Coast Guardsman H. C. Crabb in a letter to his sentry dog's owner)

Rolf, a boxer, was on sentry duty at a war plant in Boston, Massachusetts, when he alerted to the presence of a prowler. "Attack!" his master told him. Rolf captured the man and, despite a struggle, held onto him until he could be taken by his police guard handler. The officer searched the intruder and found he was carrying complete plans for the destruction of the factory.

On the West Coast, a Dalmatian doing sentry duty at a shipping-out point alerted to a saboteur who was *underneath* the pier he was patrolling. The man had slid unnoticed under the pier in his rowboat. He carried a bundle of oil-soaked rags.

And he would have caused millions of dollars worth of damage if the sentry dog had not detected what human eyes and ears could not.

Back on the East Coast, tanks awaiting shipment to Europe were being sabotaged. No one could figure out who was doing the damage. Then the military guards were given sentry dogs. During their first night on duty, the dogs caught the two men responsible.

"Our sentry dogs are doing a great job of sabotage prevention," said Colonel E. M. Daniels, chief of the Quartermaster Corps Remount Branch.

The majority of American sentry dogs employed during World War II patrolled on home turf. They guarded manufacturing plants, prisoners, and ports. They helped the Coast Guard patrol the Atlantic, Pacific, and Gulf coasts. According to the Coast Guard's Historian's Office, "the animals showed great alertness and were formidable as attackers."

These skills also led to impressive work by sentry dogs overseas.

The marines of the 28th Regiment were stationed in Iwo Jima in the South Pacific. Private First Class Raymond N. Moquin and his sentry dog, Carl, had drawn security watch. They performed this duty from a foxhole located a good distance away from the rest of the troops. To maintain communication, Moquin stretched a string from his foxhole to the hands or feet of the front line marines in the nearest foxholes.

During the night, Carl repeatedly alerted. This signal indicated the presence of a large number of enemy soldiers. Moquin pulled the string to warn the front-line marines of this danger.

A large and bloody battle followed. More than one hundred enemy soldiers lost their lives. But only two marines were wounded.

"The non-coms had time to pass the word," Moquin said of the front-line marines to whom he had tied the string. "They told me next morning that almost every man in the outfit was asleep. I hate to think of what would have happened if the signal hadn't worked." The troops were indeed lucky that the signal worked, and even luckier that Carl alerted to the enemy presence. For, without his warnings, Moquin might never have gotten a chance to use the signal.

Hey, another sentry dog that served overseas, didn't start his military career on a very good note. Before the night of December 6, 1942, Hey was best known as a dog with a particularly bad temper. On his trip to the South Pacific on an army transport ship, the German shepherd-chow cross bit twenty soldiers. Then, on that fateful night, Hey was assigned sentry duty. He and a handler were patrolling when, around midnight, Hey alerted. He went rigid. His nose quivered and pointed toward the darkness. A low growl escaped from his throat.

The sentry quietly called for help. Then he and his fellow soldiers crept in the direction Hey had indicated. Minutes later they discovered and shot a Japanese sniper sneaking through the bush. Thanks to Hey's warning, not one American soldier was harmed. The soldiers Hey had bitten began to rethink their opinion of the dog.

These are just five stories of how sentry dogs served the United States during World War II. There are many more. Of the 10,425 war dogs the United States trained during that period, 9,295 were trained as sentries, and most of these dogs served at home. Not all of their stories are as dramatic as those told above. And most pale next to the adventures of the scout and messenger dogs that served on the front lines. But sentry dogs were just as important to the security of the United States as their glamorous front-line counterparts.

On Patrol

"No patrols led by dogs were fired on first or suffered casualties." (A sentence commonly found in reports on war dog platoons)

American troops were preparing to attack the town of Umingam on Luzon, an island in the South Pacific. Before they began their raid, they wanted to find out exactly what they would be up against. Three patrols were ordered to steal into the town at night to see what they could learn. It would be a very dangerous mission.

All three patrols requested scout dogs. Only two dogs were available. One patrol had to do without.

The three patrols slipped silently into the night. The two patrols led by scout dogs made quick progress. Shadowy rice fields and pitch-black alleys didn't slow them down. They only stopped when the scout dog and its handler up ahead stopped. Then they would watch to see what the

51

dog's warning meant. It might indicate the presence of a Japanese sentry, or a native who could give them away. The troops would go around this trouble and then continue on their way.

Both dog-led patrols soon made their way into town. Once there, they quickly gathered the information they needed. Then they hurried back to American lines, arriving before dawn.

The dogless patrol wasn't so lucky. What was left of it didn't straggle back to American lines for three days. Scout dogs were clearly a valuable asset.

Scout dogs were able to give warning at anywhere from twenty to several hundred yards. The distance depended on such things as wind direction and speed, concentration of human scent , humidity, denseness or openness of country, and the handler's ability to read his dog. Even in the worst conditions, a scout dog could usually detect the presence of enemies long before its human counterparts could.

The scout dog's keen senses helped troops on the move and at rest. Their presence was so important to sleeping troops because it helped ease their fear of being taken by surprise in the night. Captain William Putney, commander of the Third War Dog Platoon, gives this example to illustrate how the troops' nighttime fears were eased by dogs.

"One night, a battalion [of marines] fired thirty-eight hundred rounds of ammunition, killing one water buffalo and wounding one marine. No enemy were known to be in the area. Dogs were called in and the next night quiet reigned."

These trained and alert scout dogs gave peace of mind because they saved lives. Here are the stories of seven scout dogs who served during World War II.

Chips

Chips was the first American dog hero of World War II. This scout dog saved countless lives when he ran through the line of fire to disarm enemy machine gunners. He did this during the American campaign to take Sicily, an island off the southern tip of Italy. Chips and his handler, Private John P. Rowell, were part of a pre-dawn landing force that hit the beach there in July 1943. They had advanced about four hundred yards when machine-gun fire began pouring out of a grass hut up ahead.

Then "things happened pretty fast," Rowell remembers. As he and the other American soldiers hit the sand, Chips bolted. The dog yanked his leash from Rowell's hand and tore towards the hut. He was inside it in a flash.

"There was an awful lot of noise," Rowell remembered. "Then I saw one fellow come out the door with Chips at his throat. I called him off before he could kill the man. Right afterward, the other fellow came out holding his hands above his head."

Rowell took the two Italian gunners prisoner.

Chips suffered a powder wound and a scalp wound in the attack. He was given medical treatment and quickly returned to duty. That night he helped Rowell capture ten more Italian soldiers.

Word of Chips' heroism spread. He was cited for performing "with utter disregard to his own safety." In November 1943, he was awarded two medals: the Silver Star for bravery and a Purple Heart for wounds received in action. These medals were later withdrawn when some people complained about an animal being given medals meant for humans. With or without his medals, though, Chips was a hero. General Dwight D. Eisenhower, then Allied Commander in Chief in the Mediterranean theater, even tried to congratulate him in person. But Eisenhower forgot what Chips did not, that dogs can only be petted by their handlers. When Eisenhower reached for him, Chips bit the four-star general's hand.

Andy

Andy landed with the marines on Bougainville, an island in the South Pacific. It was a surprise landing, and the marines knew the Japanese would try to bring in reinforcements to fight the Americans. They had to prevent these reinforcements from getting through. The only way to do that was with a roadblock.

There were two trails the Japanese could use. Andy and his handlers, Private Robert Lansley and Private Jack Mahoney, were assigned to lead two-hundred-fifty men up one of those trails. It was called the Piva Trail.

The big black Doberman was one of the few dogs in the platoon that was trusted to work off leash. He worked twenty-five yards ahead of the column of marines. If Andy got too far ahead, Lansley made a clucking sound and motioned for Andy to drop back.

It was rough going. The Piva didn't seem like much of a trail. The marines had to cut their way through the dense jungle. And they had to be on constant alert against snipers.

This was where Andy's work — and the work of all scout dogs — was so important. The jungle offered almost foolproof camouflage against human detection. But it couldn't fool a scout dog's trained and sensitive nose and ears.

During the march, Andy would run happily along until he sensed something unusual, something that threatened danger. Then he would freeze. The hair on his neck and back would stand on end.

When Andy stopped short, the marines knew to drop to the ground. They learned to drop quickly.

Once when Andy alerted, the Japanese ambush started firing a machine gun. Its bullets missed Lansley and Mahoney by only two feet. If not for Andy's warning, these two marines and many others could have been killed. Andy alerted two other times during that trip up the trail. Both times, the men took cover. Then they surrounded and eliminated the enemy patrols.

That day, Andy's company advanced further than any other company and occupied the only major position captured by the Americans. Not one marine was killed or wounded during the march.

Andy served on many other patrols. On day fourteen of the operation, he performed what Lieutenant Clyde Henderson, commander of the First Marine Dog Platoon, called one of the most extraordinary feats of the Bougainville campaign.

An American advance had been held up for some time by machine-gun fire. No one knew where the Japanese were firing from. Lansley and Mahoney volunteered to take Andy and try to help their fellow marines.

With Andy in the lead, the two soldiers headed into the jungle. When Andy froze this time, however, he wasn't so easy to read. He seemed confused. He turned sideways and moved in a way that usually indicated there were strangers ahead. Then he pointed to the left. Then he pointed to the right.

Lansley told Mahoney to cover him. Then he crawled up beside Andy. He peeked through the foliage. All he could see was a small trail with a banyan tree to the left of it and a banyan tree to the right. Lansley studied both trees. The leaves didn't look unusual. But the bushes hiding the trees' roots looked odd. He quickly guessed that the bushes were camouflaged machine-gun nests. They had been placed on the left and right of the trail in order to create a deadly cross fire.

The marine sprayed the base of each tree with machine-gun fire. Then he ran forward and hurled grenades into the dugouts he found beneath each tree. Lansley and the men who followed him destroyed this deadly trap. The troops could then move forward.

Andy was a hero.

Barron

"If Barron hadn't given me the signal that time, I'd still be lying in that trench, and so would a lot of other guys," said Joseph C. Coates, a marine private in the Second World War.

The marines were fighting on Motobu Peninsula, on the Japanese island of Okinawa. Barron and Coates, his handler, were leading the company's advance across the peninsula when the dog alerted. The marines dropped into abandoned Japanese trenches.

The Japanese had been waiting to ambush the

Americans. When the Americans halted their advance, the Japanese came out and attacked. The marines fought from the trenches and drove the Japanese back.

But the battle wasn't over yet. Coates was lying in a trench next to Barron when he felt the dog's hair stand on end. He heard him growl. The marine looked to the side and saw a column of Japanese soldiers trying to sneak up on them. He stood and shot at the soldier in the lead. The other marines starting firing and the enemy quickly retreated.

Boy

This scout dog served with the marines on the islands of Peleliu and Okinawa. Twice he alerted to Japanese ambushes in time for his fellow soldiers to avoid bloodshed. A third time, however, his alert was too late. The marines had gotten too close to where the Japanese were hiding. As Boy started to alert, the Japanese opened fire.

But Boy refused to let the Japanese get the better of his troops. He tore away from his handler and, racing through thick underbrush, charged the enemy gun.

During his charge, this devildog, as marine canines were often called, took a bullet in his left foreshoulder. But his action surprised the Japanese. And it bought the marines the minutes they needed to capture and silence the Japanese gun.

Stubby

WWI trench war dog

Coastguardsman and guard dog

"Dogs for Defense" poster

Caesar receives a message

Caesar wounded

War dog in training

Attack on command

Sentry duty

Chips meets General Eisenhower

Andy

Devildogs

Sled dogs in training

Nemo

After the battle, Boy was treated like any other brave soldier. The marines gently put the dog on a stretcher and put him in an ambulance. Then he was driven to an emergency first-aid station where a navy surgeon treated his wound.

Rolo

Rolo was one of the first six dogs to join the Marine Corps. He was also one of the first to lose his life in battle.

During his first two months on Bougainville, the Doberman and his handlers, Private Russell T. Friedrich and Private James M. White, successfully led a number of patrols. Rolo was considered an excellent scout dog and was trusted to work off leash.

Rolo lost his life during an assignment to point Japanese positions in the jungle for an army unit temporarily attached to the marines. He and Friedrich were leading a good distance ahead of the patrol when Rolo alerted. But the patrol leader did not believe the dog's alert. He insisted that Rolo and Friedrich continue into the jungle. They walked right into a trap.

"We could hear the Japs hollering, 'Doggie, doggie!' and then chattering something in Japanese we took to mean 'dog,'" White remembered. They "were intent on getting the dog...."

Friedrich sent Rolo to White, where he hoped

he'd be out of danger. But the gunfire grew more intense. And much of it was directed at Rolo.

"The bullets as they cross-fired kept coming closer to us," White said. "I was debating how to get out. Friedrich was only eight feet from me, but behind a tree. I sent Rolo to him as the bullets came closer.

"Just as Rolo got to Friedrich, he was hit.

"Rolo whined a minute and then died."

Friedrich was also shot during this deadly battle and White narrowly escaped death. A Japanese bullet tore through his helmet and just grazed his scalp.

The men were forced to retreat. When they returned, they found Rolo's body, but Friedrich was gone, presumably taken as a prisoner of war.

Wolf

As Wolf led the infantry patrol through the Corabello Mountains in Northern Luzon, an island in the Philippines, he scented the enemy. Luckily for the Americans, Wolf scented at quite a distance. The Japanese were on a hill about 150 yards away. The patrol had time to take cover before the Japanese attacked.

Wolf was wounded during the fighting that followed. Pieces of shell tore through the German shepherd's coat. But the brave dog didn't cry out. He didn't show any signs of pain. The men around him never even knew he had been hurt.

As the battle raged on, the Americans realized they were outnumbered. They had to turn back before it was too late. But the Japanese nearly had them surrounded. It would be tough to break through enemy lines and return safely to head-quarters.

Again, Wolf and his handler took the lead. Three times Wolf alerted the patrol to Japanese troops closing in on it, and each time the Americans successfully avoided coming into contact with the enemy. Thanks in large part to Wolf's alerts, the American troops arrived back at their camp without a single casualty.

But it wasn't an entirely happy ending. Once back at camp, the men discovered Wolf's wounds. A veterinarian performed an emergency operation, but was unable to save Wolf's life. The 25th Division casualty list includes, among others: WOLF, US Army War Dog, T121, Died of Wounds — Wounded in Action.

Peefke

Most scout dogs saw action in the Pacific, though some worked in the European theater, as it was called. One of these dogs was a German shepherd named Peefke.

Peefke led patrols of American troops through the Italian Alps. It was slow, hard work. The dog often warned of enemy ambushes in these mountains.

One day Peefke alerted on an empty trail. Where was the enemy? The dog's handler looked around but saw no enemy troops. Then he looked down and saw something the enemy had left behind. It was a trip wire. The wire was attached to three mines that could have destroyed the entire American patrol. Peefke's warning allowed the Americans to destroy the mines instead of being destroyed by them.

Because of Peefke, countless soldiers would go home alive at the end of the war. Peefke would not be one of these soldiers, however. On March 20, 1945, the dog was hit by an enemy hand grenade and killed in action.

Messenger Dogs

"Jack was the means of bringing help to his master." (from a letter sent by General Thomas Holcomb, commandant of the Marine Corps, to Jack's previous owner)

During World War II, dogs provided an important link between troops in the field and at headquarters. This link had to be maintained at all times, and sometimes messenger dogs were the only way to maintain it. Other means of communication often failed. Telephone lines weren't laid or were cut by the enemy. Walkie-talkies failed in the dense jungle. It was too dangerous to send human runners. And smoke, fog, or darkness grounded carrier pigeons. But very little stopped messenger dogs from getting through.

The dogs were fast. They could cover up to five miles of broken ground over shell holes, through mud, under bushes, across water, and over barbed wire in about half the time it would take a man to cover the same course. (The dogs were clocked at one mile in four minutes over rough terrain.) Their speed, combined with their size and the fact that they traveled low to the ground, made them more difficult targets than human runners. And because of their keen sense of smell, the dogs were able to deliver messages to camps that had moved.

Messenger dogs helped maintain communication in another way — by laying telephone wire. An instrument and one end of the wire were attached to the dog. A man in the trenches would hold the reel. The wire would unwind as the dog raced to the advance outpost, laying a half-mile of wire in just five minutes.

Messenger dogs saved lives. They relieved human soldiers of very dangerous jobs. They got urgent messages through quickly. And they carried urgently needed supplies.

One dog who carried a life-saving message for reinforcements and stretcher carriers was Jack, a Belgian shepherd who landed with the marines on Bougainville.

Jack had been left at an animal shelter in Jamaica, New York, by an army inductee. When Joseph Verhaeghe stopped by the shelter to look for a dog for his son, Bobby, he was delighted to find Jack. The dog quickly became part of the family.

When the United States entered the war, Verhaeghe tried to enlist in the service. But he was turned down because he had a punctured eardrum. Then Verhaeghe heard about Dogs for Defense. He figured that even if he couldn't fight for his country, Jack could. Verhaeghe talked to his wife about it. "You'll have to ask Bobby," she told him.

Verhaeghe talked to his son about donating Jack to Dogs for Defense. Bobby didn't know what to do. He didn't want to lose his pet. But he wanted to do what was right. In the end, Bobby made the unselfish choice.

"If Jack can save lives, I want him to go in," Bobby told his dad.

Verhaeghe took Jack to a Dogs for Defense induction center on Hicksville, Long Island.

"He wanted to go when I started to leave," Verhaeghe said. "But I told him to stay and he seemed to know that he was there for some purpose." That purpose became clear during the November 1, 1943, invasion of Bougainville.

It was the seventh day of the invasion. Jack and one of his handlers, Private Gordon J. Wortman, were assigned to a marine roadblock far inside the jungle. When the Japanese viciously attacked the roadblock, the unit's future looked bleak. The isolated group of marines began to suffer casualties. Wortman received a crippling wound to the leg. Jack was shot in the back.

The officer in charge knew that without reinforcements and first aid he would lose his entire company. But the Japanese had cut the phone lines that connected the roadblock to headquarters. And a human messenger would never make it through Japanese lines alive. The company's only hope was Jack.

The officer crawled over to the wounded handler and dog.

"Son, we've got to get through to headquarters. Your dog is the only one we can send. Do you think he can make it?"

"I think so, sir," Wortman said. "He's got lots of guts."

The officer quickly wrote his message on a piece of paper. He handed the paper to Wortman, who placed it inside the pouch on Jack's neck.

"This is it, old boy," Wortman said to Jack. "We're depending on you. 'Report' to Paul."

The wounded animal struggled to stand. Once on his feet, however, he seemed to gain strength. He took off in the direction of his other handler, Private Paul J. Castracane, at headquarters. The besieged marines anxiously watched their only hope dash through the hail of machine gun bullets and into the jungle.

Castracane was in his tent taking off his gear when he heard someone yell that Jack was coming into camp. When the two met, Jack collapsed at his handler's feet. Blood was gushing out of his wound. The marine quickly removed the message from Jack's pouch and ran it over to his commanding officer. Then he returned and gently carried Jack to a first-aid station.

While Jack's wound was being cared for, marine reinforcements were rushing to the roadblock. They quickly trapped the attacking Japanese. Then stretcher bearers hurried to the scene to tend to the wounded American soldiers.

Jack saved many lives that day, including his own and Wortman's. The marine was not surprised to owe his life to his dog. In a letter he wrote to his parents less than a month before being wounded, Wortman wrote, "Don't worry about me. Jack will take care of me."

Rescue Dogs

"They saved many lives and gave soldiers great contentment." (World War II war dog trainer)

When a British bomber hit bad weather over Greenland, the crew was forced to land the plane on thin ice in a remote area. There were no other humans within five hundred miles. The crew immediately started making SOS calls. Luckily, a U.S. Navy ship picked up the downed aircraft's distress signals. The ship then radioed the Air Transport Command of the U.S. Army for help.

Dogs, drivers, sledges, and other necessary equipment were quickly loaded onto a transport plane. The sled dog team was then flown as close to the downed aircraft as possible. Once on the ground, the drivers harnessed and hitched their dogs. Then, with a crack of the whip, they rushed to the downed plane.

The team quickly saw to the well-being of the aircraft's crew. Then it salvaged some valuable equipment from the airplane. The team then rushed the crew and the equipment back to the transport, which carried them to safety. As for the downed bomber — it broke through the ice and sank.

Sled Dogs

Thousands of planes were flown directly from the United States to Great Britain and Russia during World War II. Not a few of them went down over the ice-covered Arctic. The Air Transport Command of the U.S. Army had sled dog teams scattered throughout the North Atlantic to make sure the crew of downed planes didn't freeze to death. Three hundred dogs and their handlers were stationed in such remote places as northern Maine, Alaska, Greenland, Labrador, and Newfoundland.

Most of the army's sled dogs were Alaskan huskies and malamutes. These breeds were best suited for the Arctic regions, where they did most of their work. These draft animals worked in teams. The sled dogs pulled sledges, or sleighs, over snowy and icy terrain. Their goal was usually the rescue of downed pilots. Pack dogs carried packs weighing as much as sixty-five pounds on their backs. In their packs they carried anything from food to first-aid supplies to ammunition.

Sled dogs became known for the work they did helping troubled soldiers in icy conditions. So when a call for help went out from a bloody, frozen battlefield in France, the sled dogs of the Air Transport Command were the answer.

This was the Battle of the Bulge, one of the bloodiest battles of World War II. It was also one of the most frustrating for rescue workers. Bitter cold and heavy snowfall got in the way of their rescue efforts. Stretcher bearers could barely trudge through the hip-deep snow. Ambulances could not plow through the tall snow drifts. Wounded soldiers were dying on the front lines from lack of medical care. Something had to be done to help these men.

Then an urgent call was made for dogs — sled dogs.

Twenty-three sled dog teams received orders over their two-way radio sets to help in the rescue efforts at the Battle of the Bulge. These teams were stationed all over the Arctic Circle. Now these far-flung teams had to be quickly gathered and ferried across the Atlantic to France, where the battle was taking place.

C-45 airplanes picked up the individual teams — drivers and dogs — from their remote stations. These smaller planes brought the teams to three large four-motored transport planes. These big birds were set to take the dogs and their handlers across the Atlantic.

The eighty-pound dogs were chained to the planes' bucket seats. This was done to prevent them from fighting with each other during the long overseas flight. As an added safety measure, the pilots flew at eleven thousand feet. The lack of oxygen at this altitude kept all but a couple of the dogs too drowsy to fight.

The first planeload of drivers, dogs, sledges, and other equipment arrived just four days after the order for dogs went out. A total of 209 dogs were brought together to help in the rescue efforts at the Battle of the Bulge.

Casualty Dogs

Another type of dog that performed rescue work was the war casualty dog. Also known as ambulance dogs or Red Cross dogs, war casualty dogs were trained to locate wounded soldiers on the front lines and report their whereabouts to first-aid detachments. These dogs located many soldiers whom their human counterparts missed.

The safest time to search for wounded soldiers was at night. Since lights attracted the enemy's attention, not to mention fire, the search often had to be made in total darkness. Under such conditions, it was easy to overlook men who had crawled behind rocks or into holes for safety and were now unable or afraid to call out for help. Only dogs, whose keen noses could pick up the smell of blood, readily found these soldiers.

A Russian soldier recalled what it was like to be saved by one of these dogs.

The soldier was critically injured while taking cover under some bushes. He knew he needed immediate medical attention, but, he wondered, how would the first-aid crew find him beneath the brush and the rubble? He didn't have the energy to call out to them. He was unable to make any kind of movement that might attract their attention. The soldier thought that he would surely bleed to death.

Thus the man was startled when he felt something cold and wet on the back of his neck. He struggled to turn his head. What he saw was a big dog, an Alsatian. The dog wore a canvas pack around his middle. The pack was emblazoned with the Red Cross emblem. For the first time, the man felt a glimmer of hope.

Within moments, the man began to lose consciousness. He was aware of very few things. Flashlights. Stretcher bearers. And a big dog standing in the distance.

That particular dog was Bob, one of six casualty dogs working with the first-aid crew. His running and jumping told them that he had found a wounded man. (Some dogs took a stick that was tied around their necks into their mouths to show they had made a find.) The first-aid crew followed Bob back to the wounded soldier.

All totaled, Bob found seventeen wounded men that night. These were all men that the first-aid crew had missed.

Dogs and Explosives

"Dogs are a weapon." (a World War II officer)

Two other types of dogs were used for a short while during World War II. They were mine-detection dogs, or M-dogs, and anti-tank dogs.

M-dogs were trained to locate deadly mines planted by the enemy. The army based its training on the dog's ability to find buried bones. The animals worked on a six-foot leash. They were trained to alert to the presence of a mine at a distance of one to four yards. They were also trained to indicate mine-free areas that were safe to pass.

In training, M-dogs performed extremely well. But they were unable to repeat that performance on the front lines. When the dogs were sent to North Africa, they were so distracted by battle-field conditions that their performance fell dramatically. They were able to detect only about half of the mines in front of them. The army decided that anything less than a ninety percent success rate was unacceptable. The M-dog units were deactivated and mine-dog training was discontinued.

Not all M-dogs fared so poorly, however. In Russia, a mongrel named Zucha was said to have found two thousand mines in eighteen days. The dog was used to de-mine hundreds of miles of railroad tracks and several key airports.

While Zucha's job was to help get rid of explosives, other Russian dogs were employed in detonating them. These were the Russian anti-tank dogs.

The job of the anti-tank dogs was to destroy the enemy's tanks. These dogs carried bombs as they rushed attacking tanks. They expected to find food under the tanks. Instead, they found death. As a tank crushed the dogs, the explosives were triggered, and the tank was destroyed.

Anti-tank dogs succeeded in harming and frightening the enemy. In one early attack, these dogs destroyed nine heavy tanks and two armored cars. During a later attack, German tanks actually slowed down and turned around when they saw fifty anti-tank dogs headed in their direction.

The Russian High Command stopped using these dogs not long after they started. They didn't stop for humane reasons, although soldiers were horrified watching such carnage. Rather, the use of anti-tank dogs was stopped because they didn't harm only the enemy. It seemed the dogs would run under *any* tank, German or Russian.

Coming Home

"I want to thank you for the wonderful dog you returned to us." (from a letter Mrs. Herbert E. Allen of Washington sent to the Quartermaster General)

At the end of World War II, the Army, Coast Guard, and Marines had several thousand dogs in their service. Most of these K-9s were eventually returned to civilian life. But first they had to undergo what the services called "processing in reverse." This detraining took almost as long as the original training it was meant to reverse. Handlers taught their dogs that all human beings were friends. Different men talked to, petted, and played with the dogs. Many handlers wore civilian clothes instead of military uniforms.

To check the progress of this detraining, veteran canines were placed in situations where they previously would have attacked. Aggravators again taunted them with sticks and verbal abuse.

Now, however, the dogs were told *not* to attack. Dogs that responded with friendliness rather than viciousness were considered detrained.

After giving them a final physical exam, the army shipped detrained dogs home at government expense. Certificates of faithful service and honorable discharge were sent along with a kit containing the dog's collar, leash, and a copy of the War Department's manual, *War Dogs*.

Although these animals were now fit for civilian life, they had not been totally detrained. The commands "heel," "sit," "down," and "stay" were reinforced up until discharge. Most owners were pleasantly surprised to get back such obedient dogs. Many of them wrote to the army to express their thanks. Here is an excerpt from a letter one woman wrote:

> "I want to thank you for the wonderful dog you returned to us. Smarty is a perfect example of health and alertness and she was so eager to show us her obedience commands that we understood them even before the instructions arrived two days late. It was a genuine sacrifice for Herbie to donate his dog to the armed forces, but now he is receiving his reward by receiving a dog more beautiful and better trained than he ever thought possible."

Other owners were surprised — and grateful — that their pets had not been turned into vicious attack dogs. One woman wrote to the army:

"Our dog has benefitted by his year in the army and since his return, has been as gentle and friendly and loving as before.... Many people were under the impression that he would be a vicious animal on his return, but that is definitely not so. We are very proud of our returned veteran."

Not all dogs were returned to their original owners. Some dogs were from pounds or had owners who were no longer able to care for them. Dogs for Defense volunteered to find homes for these dogs. The organization had thousands of requests for them. It gave preference to World War II veterans and owners of dogs who had died in the service.

Many dog handlers requested permission from the dog's previous owners to keep their dogs after the war. One marine wrote:

"During the past months Judy and I have been through a lot together and I have become very fond of her. I would like to have her after the war. So if you can possibly see your way clear to part with her I would be forever grateful to you ... and would pay any amount I could afford if I could have her."

The owner's answer was usually "Yes."

The army held onto a small number of dogs for breeding and for peacetime duties.

And a small number of dogs had to be put to sleep. These were dogs that, despite repeated attempts, could not be detrained. They were too jumpy, nervous, or aggressive to be returned safely to civilian life.

Finally, there were hundreds of dogs who never returned from World War II. Most died from disease. The rest were killed or fatally wounded in action.

War Dogs Since World War II

"Military dogs today are very important for the security of the United States." (Colonel Gary L. Stamp, Director, Department of Defense Military Dog Veterinary Service)

War dogs came into their own during World War II. More dogs — 250,000 in all — were used during this war than in any war before or since. With its new war dog program, the United States joined its allies — England and Russia — and its enemies — Germany and Japan — in the use of war dogs.

War dogs continued to serve the United States after World War II. They were used during the Korean War, the Vietnam War, and the Gulf War, though not in as great numbers as during World War II. And they are still used to maintain security throughout the United States and around the world during times of peace.

Korean War (1950–1953)

Only one dog platoon, the 26th Infantry Scout Dog Platoon, saw service during this conflict. But, as the following excerpt from the army's General Orders shows, its record was outstanding.

"The 26th Infantry Scout Dog Platoon, during its service in Korea, has participated in hundreds of combat patrol actions by supporting the patrols with the service of an expert scout dog handler and his highly trained scout dog.... The unbroken record of faithful and gallant performances of these missions by the individual handlers and their dogs in support of patrols has saved countless casualties through giving early warning to the friendly patrol of threats to its security.... Throughout its long period of difficult and hazardous service, the 26th Infantry Scout Dog Platoon has never failed those with whom it served, has consistently shown outstanding devotion to duty ... and has won on the battlefield a degree of respect and admiration which has established it as a unit of the greatest importance to the Eighth United States Army."

The war dogs were so popular that patrols did not want to go out without them. But with just one dog platoon consisting of twenty-seven dogs in service, it was impossible to give every patrol a dog.

A request was made and granted that a scout dog platoon be assigned to each division in Korea. Peace talks began before these five additional platoons could be trained and shipped, however.

Vietnam War (1957–1975)

The two thousand dogs that worked as scouts, sentries, and patrol dogs during the Vietnam War were credited with saving more than ten thousand lives. The most famous of these dogs was Nemo.

Nemo was one of hundreds of sentry dogs that helped to protect American air bases inside Vietnam during the Vietnam War. Air Force and Marine Corps fighters, fighter bombers, and transport planes worked from these bases. This made them an important target of the enemy.

On December 5, 1966, Nemo and his handler, Airman Second Class Robert Thorneberg, were patrolling Tan Son Nhut air base near an old Vietnamese cemetery. After a deadly attack by the Vietcong the night before, neither dog nor handler could be too careful.

Shortly before midnight, Nemo paused by a Japanese shrine. It was a clear, starlit night, and

Thorneberg had no trouble reading his dog's signals. Nemo's eyes were glistening. His ears had perked up. And the fur around his neck was standing on end. The enemy was nearby.

Thorneberg put Nemo on alert. "Watch him!" the marine commanded. As he spoke, the hidden enemy opened fire. One bullet tore through Thorneberg's shoulder. Another entered Nemo's skull under his right eye and exited through his muzzle.

"Get him!" Thorneberg ordered, letting go of Nemo's leash. The wounded dog leapt into the darkness. Human screams told Thorneberg that Nemo had hit his mark. The handler quickly called for help before rejoining the bloody battle.

Backup troops arrived to find Nemo, bloodied but alive, standing guard over his handler. Thorneberg was unconscious from bullet wounds to the shoulder and the arm. Two Vietcong guerrillas lay nearby. One was dead from dog-bite wounds. The other from bite and bullet wounds. Four abandoned machine guns showed that Nemo and Thorneberg had frightened away two other attackers.

Nemo had saved Thorneberg's life. He also saved many other lives and aircraft, which could have been lost if the attack had not been stopped.

Nemo received a hero's welcome when he returned to the United States in July 1967. The dog who lost his eye but saved so much more retired to

Lackland Air Force Base, Texas. There he became a symbol of the important relationship between dog and handler.

Persian Gulf War (1991)

Biber and his handler, Sergeant Roger Loraditch, were one of four teams that worked anti-terrorist duty during this Middle East conflict. The teams did security checks at gates and searched the military base in Dhahran, Saudi Arabia, among other targets. During his searches, Biber discovered several explosives. These included a live hand grenade that had been placed beneath his master's cot and three grenades at the Kuwait City Airport.

Biber was also wounded in action. He cut his right front paw during a search of the U.S. Embassy in Kuwait City on the day of the cease-fire, February 27, 1991. Seven stitches were needed to close the wound.

Peacetime

There are two thousand United States military working dogs on active duty around the world today. Most of these dogs and their handlers patrol American military bases throughout the U.S. and overseas. Others help the Secret Service protect the President, Vice President, their families, and foreign dignitaries. In 1994, military working dogs performed 115 explosives checks for the

President alone. Still other military working dogs assist the Department of the U.S. Treasury's Customs Service, the Federal Aviation Administration (FAA), and the U.S. Border Patrol. Military working dogs perform explosives- and drug-detection work for these agencies.

All of the Department of Defense's military working dogs and handlers are trained by the Air Force at Lackland Air Force Base in Texas. (The Air Force took over that job from the Army in 1958.) The Air Force's 341st Training Squadron also trains dogs and handlers for the FAA, the Secret Service, Customs, and Border Patrol.

The Dog Training Center looks at hundreds of dogs before it chooses the 250 or so it will train each year. All of these dogs come from vendors or breeders. Most are Belgian Malinois (a shepherd type), German shepherds, sporting breeds such as Labradors and other retrievers, and a few mixed breeds. The Department of Defense has five smaller dogs — four beagles and one Cairn terrier — for searching small places such as ships and airplane cockpits.

All dogs are trained in perimeter patrol. All are trained to be aggressive. All, that is, except for those slated for the Federal Aviation Administration (FAA). This organization uses its dogs at airports amid lots of people and wants the animals to be friendly rather than aggressive.

After learning perimeter patrol, the dogs are trained to detect either explosives *or* drugs. It has to be one or the other because a federal officer wouldn't want to handle a suitcase full of explosives in the same way he or she would handle a suitcase full of drugs.

Not all military working dogs are sent to guard military bases or to assist the FAA, Secret Service, Customs, or Border Patrol. Some are sent on special assignment. One such assignment included the World Trade Center bombing trials. Military working dogs and their handlers were sent to New York City to support local law enforcement in explosives detection at the courthouse. With their thorough training and sharp senses, these K-9s are a terrorist's worst nightmare.

Epilogue

When soldiers were remembered during the 50th anniversary of the end of World War II, war dogs were not forgotten. A United States memorial to heroic war dogs was unveiled at Naval Station Guam in July 1994, the 50th anniversary of that island's liberation.

"The fact that these dogs were killed instead of us and kept us from ever being ambushed or surprised at night makes them heroes in my mind," said Dr. William Putney. The veterinarian, who commanded the marines Third War Dog Platoon on Guam, helped get the monument erected.

Twenty-four dogs died and were buried at the War Dog Cemetery on Guam. Their names will be inscribed on the granite memorial.

A bronze life-size sculpture of a Doberman was placed atop the memorial. Its title describes how soldiers throughout history have felt about their canine companions: "Always Faithful."

Fun Facts
about War Dogs

About World War II . . .

The U.S. War Dog Program unofficially became known as the K-9 Corps because "K-9" sounds like "canine."

The Army tried to dye Dalmatians khaki so that they wouldn't stand out so much on the front lines. It didn't work — the dogs' hides just faded to splotchiness.

Irish setters and other bird dogs were tried on the front lines on New Guinea but failed because they pointed more parakeets than Japanese soldiers.

Many of the men but none of the dogs of the First Marine War Dog Platoon got seasick during the eighteen-day voyage to the South Pacific.

It was estimated that nearly one hundred thousand letters were written by owners anxious to learn about the dogs they had donated to their country.

The only soldiers who didn't wear dog tags were dogs.

Marine dogs were called "devildogs." Germans gave this name to the tough marines they fought against during World War I.

The marines promoted their devildogs based on length of service. If a dog had served long enough, it could outrank its master!

In "General" . . .

The War Department named the German shepherd the official U.S. Army dog in 1946.

A German shepherd's hearing ability is about twenty times better than man's.

During the Vietnam War, the enemy feared scout dogs so much that they were reportedly ordered to shoot dogs first and handlers second.

Sentry dogs have been called "guided muzzles."

This song was written about war dogs during World War II.

The K-9 Corps Song
by Arthur Roland*

From the kennels of the country,
From the homes and firesides, too;
We have joined the canine army,
Our nation's work to do;

We serve with men in battle,
And scout through jungles dense;
We are proud to be enlisted
In the cause for the Dogs for Defense;

Through the watches of the darkest night
We are ever standing alert;
And if danger comes we stick by our men,
All the rights of the flag we assert;

So bare our fangs in man's behalf
And the cause he's fighting for;
We are glad to serve as members
Of Uncle Sam's trappy, scrappy K-9 Corps.

*© 1943, by Roland Kilbon, assigned to Dogs for Defense, Inc.